Gargoyle Redemption

Laura Hawks

ACKNOWLEDGMENTS

I would like to thank all of my friends, family, and fans who sent good wishes and kept me in their thoughts during my medical crisis of late. Without your thoughts and prayers, this book might not have been published.

I would like to thank all of you for your notes, emails, and posts. They are greatly appreciated. I hope that after reading this novel, you will take the time to let me know your thoughts.

My platforms are located in the back of this book under About the Author.

I would also appreciate it very much if you left a review on Amazon and/or Goodreads.

Thank you for your patronage and friendship.

Read, Review, and Repeat

Further Reading:
Words For Warriors II: A Word Search Book
Balconies of New Orleans

YA Paranormal:
Gumshoe and the Mysterious Mushrooms
Gumshoe Goes to a Quinceanera

(These books are Adult Themed)
Demon Trilogy: Demon's Kiss
                Demon's Dream
                Demon's Web

Spirit Walker's Thrillers: Shifter's Hope
                            Shifter's Pride
                            Shifter's Journey
                            Shifter's Dance

Ghost and the Grimoire
Serena
Gargoyle Redemption

Fractured Fairytales: Snow White and the Seven Cannibals
                        The Merman and the Pirate

Valley View Mysteries: Flaming Retribution
                        Stalking the Stalker

Laura Hawks

Prologue

Darkness. It was beyond black. He couldn't even see the hand in front of his face, and Byron James did try. He felt a coldness creep into his bones. Byron was anxiously anticipating what might occur and had to get out of wherever he was. He tried to find a wall, and when he did, he yanked his hand back immediately. The wall was cold, slimy, almost like the inside of some great beast, and he was sure he felt the tentacles of something reach for him in the process.

His heart raced as he turned in circles, trying to find a way out. He wasn't even sure how he got here, but he had to get out. He had to get home. It didn't matter anymore. With hands outstretched, he ran and hoped he was going in the right direction. Byron eventually tired out, moving to a slow jog, then a walk, before he finally stopped to catch his breath and immediately felt things crawling all over him.

Desperately, he tried to brush them off, but they seemed to climb up on him faster than he could swipe them away. He was instantly reminded of the scene in

The Mummy where the scarabs consumed a person, and he was sure the same was about to happen to him. He assumed that if he stayed still, they would, so after one final massive swipe, he began to run again. Whatever it might be, he knew they couldn't crawl upon him if he were moving.

Up ahead, he saw light. He smiled as he continued moving. He found the way out of this nightmarish place. However, as he quickened his pace in his hurry to get to freedom, he ran into a webbing, and suddenly, he was entangled among the fine, spidery-filament webbing with hundreds of spiders crawling all over him, biting him.

A scream startled him until he realized it was him screaming, and he woke up, sitting amidst a pool of his own sweat, his heart pounding so much it felt like it was going to come out of his chest.

Rubbing his hand over his face, he tossed the covers off and superstitiously checked to make sure there were no spiders or anything else crawling over him. Once satisfied it had all been a dream, he headed to the bathroom. Peering at himself in the mirror, he looked pale and waned. His dark hair was askew, and his normally bright blue eyes were dull and red with weariness. His tall frame was slightly hunched over from no rest. He hadn't been getting any sleep since his trip to Ireland. At first, he just thought the lack of sleep was a result of the time changes, but it had been a week now, and still, the nightmares kept haunting him.

He was becoming apprehensive about going to sleep, yet he was so tired. He was beginning to believe that the last day in Ireland was his downfall. He had been warned about the fairy rings and fairy trees. "Such a load of malarkey," he said to the others. "There are no such things as fairies or wee folk." He laughed, and to prove it, he took a stone from the fairy ring and stuck it in his pocket.

Yet, since then, he has had a run of bad luck to go with the nightmares. First, his plane home was delayed by a full day for engine problems, then a flat tire, and finally a gas leak. There were no hotels by the airport. The closest availability was three hours away and if he went there, he would just have enough time to wash his face and come back to the airport, only to sit and wait further. The meals he was able to get were of poor quality or cold. His carry-on was stolen while he caught a couple of restless, uncomfortable snoozes. When he finally did make it to the United States, there were some questions about the contents of his suitcase and it took so long to clear immigration that he missed his connecting flight. Three days later, he finally arrived at his little bungalow in Lombard, Illinois.

He was starting to believe he was cursed, and if he believed in curses, then he had to assume he was cursed by the fairy people for taking the stone. He had hoped that if he sent the stone back to Ireland and asked someone to put it back in the ring, his bad luck would change.

However, the nightmares just continued to worsen over the past week. He was becoming irritable, angry over the littlest of annoyances, which was so unlike him. He was usually the calmest, most even-tempered man one would care to meet. Lack of sleep would wear down anyone, and he was getting extremely tired. He had to wonder if the tour guide he'd sent the stone to wouldn't touch it and, therefore, didn't return the rock back to its proper place.

As his horrible dreams persisted, Byron wondered

if he'd die with the curse over his head. Maybe once he'd angered the fairies, he'd be haunted for the rest of his days. A part of him still thought of this as superstition, but too many things had occurred to completely deny it. Each day, a wave of bad luck would get him, from something as simple as leaving his coffee on the roof of his car only to splash over his rear window so he couldn't see as he backed out and ended up hitting another vehicle, to having his computer crash and losing all of his work. True, it could be coincidental, but there were just so many instances that a part of him knew a lot of it could just be a result of his exhaustion.

Byron's nightmares varied each night with something different. The first horrendous dream he'd had, he was still in Ireland.

"Thief! Thief!" He heard as he was running, feeling as though something was chasing him, hunting him, although he couldn't see what it was. The dream had started out with him standing by the fairy ring. As he stared at it, a cold chill ran through him. He felt like he was being watched. Then something whizzed by his head, startling him. His adrenaline kicked in, and he knew he had to rapidly get away.

He ran as fast as he could, but he couldn't seem to get very far. He entered the woods only to come out in a clearing containing the exact fairy ring. "Thief!" As he ran, he could hear heavy footsteps behind him with a slight fluttering sound he couldn't quite place other than the sound of a fly when it was near his ear.

"Thief!"

He panicked further and kept running in circles. Each time he got back to the fairy ring, the footsteps seemed closer, yet he saw no one. Every time, the cry reverberated around him. "Thief!"

In a frenzied terror, he awoke, his heart still racing, his skin clammy from his night excursions. He couldn't sleep anymore and walked around his room until the sun rose and he could head to the airport to come home. If only he knew better then. He would have returned the stone immediately. To him, it was a bunch of foolishness. Still, he began to doubt his own sanity.

His nightly torment continued each time he drifted into a restless slumber. The calls of 'thief' subsided only to be replaced by other imagined terrors. One time, he was covered in bees that kept stinging him no matter how hard he tried to escape. Another time, he fell into a pit trying to escape the woods, only to keep falling into the inky dark. Still, another time, he was in a beautiful forest but fell into quicksand. Byron couldn't get out with no one around to help him as he sank deeper and deeper; his oxygen slowly being cut off. Each time, he awoke in a sweat, drenched from whatever battles he had been fighting in his slumber. Each time, he heard the word 'thief' whispered in the background just moments before he would awaken.

He didn't know where to turn to for help or what would be able to help him defeat this curse that he seemed to be under. Maybe he should go back to Ireland and to the fairy ring after all, then beg their forgiveness, but he didn't have the stone any longer and wasn't sure where it was or even if someone was kind enough to return it to its proper place. Worse, there was a part of him that still believed it was just a powerful suggestion about the fairies' curse that he was living and not an actual thing, but lack of sleep had him questioning his rationality. He could only hope that the nightmares would eventually disappear on their own, and he would get his restful slumber and life back.

Chapter One

The dark clouds covered the sky, a low rumbling following a small flash of light erupted piercing the dismal heavens. The air was heavy, laden with the rains that were about to descend from above.

Byron had felt too exhausted to drive and the morning had started out to be a beautiful summer day. He knew his reflexes wouldn't be up to handling the complexities of driving and walking to work seemed to be the perfect thing to help him wake up.

He hadn't known that the rain would be moving in throughout the day so that by the time he was ready to walk home, the clouds threatened to open up releasing the moisture in the air.

"A good walk will help me wake up." he thought as he headed out in the morning.

If only he had known about the thunderstorm brewing on the horizon when he left the house, but then, that was Chicago weather for you. Wait five minutes and it will change without warning.

Stopping to buy an umbrella from the convenience store in the building where he worked, he headed for home. It was about a mile, an easy stroll and a good stretch of the legs, but he'd barely gone two blocks when the upper atmosphere decided that was a good time to let loose the winds and rain.

Swiftly opening up the new umbrella, the wind whipped around in such a way as to turn his protection from the elements inside out just as it started to pour.

"Will nothing go my way?" Byron grumbled to himself.

He was immediately soaked. Running for cover under an awning, Byron found himself dismayed as the awning tore from the strong wind, dumping buckets of water on his head resulting in Byron immediately being drenched.

With no recourse, he ducked into the store he had originally hoped to seek refuge from before the awning was split at the seams, standing in the doorway as he shook off the excess water.

The clerk behind the register peered at him over his spectacles. He was balding on the top, his brown eyes weary with age, but a slight smirk twitched at the corners of his thin lips.

"Should've brought an umbrella, young man." his

raspy age-old voice commented, laced with a tinge of amusement.

"I had one." Byron wiped the water from his shoulders with the back of his hand before running a hand through his plastered wet hair. "It turned inside out and tore apart when I tried to open it."

The old man snorted. "Bad luck."

"I seem to have a lot of that lately."

The old man nodded as he sat back watching the sopping wet Byron who peered out the door to gaze dejectedly at the ominous weather.

"Did you want to come in more and look around? Cause you're creating a puddle at my door. Can't get any wetter if you're not wanting to stay."

"Right. Sorry." Byron thought about heading back into the storm, but the rain was really coming down hard and he just needed a break.

Slowly, he moved around the store which was filled with antiques and knick-knacks, filling every bit of retail space the building provided.

When his sloshy shoes squeaked enough and his feet squished from all the water, Byron decided to return to the storm and continue to head home.

It was then he saw it sitting in a darkened corner, almost hidden by statuettes and lamps. Byron wasn't sure what caught his eye exactly, but he couldn't resist giving it a closer look. He was going to walk past it and continue on his way, but his eyes weren't able to leave the intricately and beautifully carved piece of limestone. The features were so delicate, the feathers appeared soft as if they would flutter with a gentle breeze. He'd never seen anything carved so delicately. Try as hard as he could, he was inexplicably drawn to it.

He started to depart the establishment, but again his eyes drifted back to the exquisite stone carving. Byron was about to ask the shopkeeper how much the statue was, but realized the old proprietor could say ten thousand and he'd figure out a way to pay the amount. He just had to have it.

Striding over as if he purposely came in for this piece alone, he picked it up He was sure it was going to weigh a couple of hundred pounds, but was surprised to find it very light weight. *'It must be hollow,'* he thought, as he carried it up to the counter.

"I want this."

"Good choice. It's a unique piece. One of a kind. Came from some old building in Ireland. Usually they come from buildings in England. Despite that, this little lady has centuries of history behind her. If only she could talk, I bet she'd have some amazing stories to tell. She's approximately seven hundred and fifty years old. One such as this is rarely in such pristine condition."

Byron took out his American Express card and charged it. He was thrilled at finding such a fantastic piece. Maybe his luck was changing. He'd always thought gargoyles were intriguing but never dreamed he could actually own one.

"Can you have it delivered."

"Sorry. We don't offer that service."

"That's okay. It's lighter than I thought. I should be able to manage her alright."

"I'll be open for a couple more hours. We don't close until seven. You can go home and get a car to protect her better. Sure, this lady has been out in the rain, but in case you trip or slip, no sense busting her nose or cracking her wing off. You can set her by the door until you get back."

"That's a great idea. Thanks."

The old man reached over to the gargoyle statue and put a sold sign around the neck moments before Byron carried it over to the door.

"I'll be back as quick as I can."

Chapter Two

Byron carried the heavy gargoyle onto the porch of his house. He had a brick home, and the gargoyle would look great on top of the building. He knew they were originally made to decorate waterspouts and keep the roof from caving in with heavy rains. He couldn't resist having the statue for himself. It was one of the few things that made him smile over the past week, and finding a female gargoyle was exceptionally rare. He knew the statues were supposed to ward away evil spirits, but he didn't believe in such things. However, he hadn't believed in fairies either but had been plagued by them of late. He hoped that maybe surrounding himself with good luck charms like a gargoyle as well as any any other good luck symbol he could find, might aid him in defeating the horrors that plagued him nightly. Still, he didn't give much credence to their being able to help ward against his dreams, but he knew a part of him hoped for the best.

He didn't have time to put the gargoyle up on the roof, so he set it down while he opened the door. He was going to leave it outside on the porch, but he feared someone would take it. Hesitantly, Byron brought it inside and left it beside the entryway. When the weekend came, he would get the ladder out to put it on his rooftop, but until then, he knew it would be protected from theft.

Once he was settled in, he plopped down in front of the television with a beer in his hand. He was exhausted, and all he wanted to do was peacefully sleep without the barrage of nightmares that continually plagued him. Maybe if he got drunk enough, he would be in a stupor so strong that he wouldn't dream.

Several beers later, he couldn't keep his eyes open no matter how hard he tried. However, he had barely shut them when a bright glow seemed to encase his entire house. The brightness woke him, if he had, in fact, even fallen asleep. He tried desperately to not open his eyes, and in moments, the light was gone. Maybe it was something on the television that became bright, even though he was sure he had turned it off just minutes ago. He was too tired to care, at this point, to look for the remote again. Hell, he'd fallen asleep with the TV on before, and he was pretty sure he would do so again in the future. How often had he thought the television watched him more than he watched it?

He heard footsteps, but it hadn't really mattered to him. Again, he was sure it was just the television. Silence seemed to surround him, and soon, he was in a wooded forest. The last time he was here, he'd been in quicksand. He knew he had to move, but he didn't know where to go or why, only that his nightmare was about to commence.

"Come with me," a soft, feminine voice called from behind.

At first, Byron wondered what sort of hell she was going to bring with her. Taking a steading breath, he turned to look at her and was taken aback. Her features were tender, gentle, and kind. She held her hand out. Her nails were long and manicured. Her long bronze hair blew lightly in the slight breeze. She looked familiar, like he should know who she was, but for the life of him, he couldn't place her. However, it was her eyes that bewitched him with their rich amber color.

"Who are you?"

"You can call me Angela. Now come." She waved her fingers in a come hither motion to attempt to get him to clasp her hand.

"Byron," he said simply. "Byron James." Since there were no bugs crawling on him, he wasn't being stung, sinking in quicksand, being chased, or falling into a deep black hole, he gladly slipped his hand in hers, surprised at the cool strength she seemed to possess, and let her lead him away from the small grove he had found himself in just moments ago.

They had barely traveled a few hundred feet when they found themselves surrounded by four beautiful yet menacing figures.

Chapter Three

"Stop. You are interfering. He is ours to punish as we see fit." A male strode forward, his hands clenched at his sides. Clearly, he was the commander of the small group.

"Thief," the other three chimed in unison, held back by the stern look of the leader.

Byron had to admit they were all extremely beautiful. Even the closest male was incredibly handsome with light brown hair and silver eyes. His ears were pointed, the tips just peeking out of his long hair. The others, both male and female, that encircled them were just as stunning as the angry man who had confronted them.

The woman, whose hand Byron was still holding, pulled him closer. "He is currently under my protection. You will leave him alone."

The others laughed at her. "You're in our territory now," the handsome man said. "Leave before you start a war with us, as well. He is ours to punish for his insolence."

Byron's companion chuckled softly. "You may

rule this land, and you have set forth this punishment, but I will fight for him. I will now protect him. It is my duty."

The leader gave a quick nod and Byron hoped that meant they were going to acquiesce his companion's request to leave him alone.

However, when one of the women stepped around to the side of them, and the other woman moved to the opposite area, he realized a battle was about to ensue. The two men stepped closer together, and suddenly, all four of them sprouted wings on their backs, the gossamer appendages shimmered in the light.

Byron felt a cold shiver go down his spine. How were they to fight against fairies? They certainly weren't like what he pictured. They were as tall as humans, only their pointed ears and diaphanous wings made them different. For some reason, he was thinking of Tinker Bell-type creatures whenever he thought of fairies, small and unobtrusive.

As if reading his thoughts, Angela nodded. "When they are friendly, they are tiny and cute. Angry and ready for war, they have grown to the height of their targets. Us."

"How are we to fight them?" Byron asked. "It's my fault. I should have believed. I shouldn't have taken the stone. I tried to have it returned. Please forgive me." He looked at the four fairies, his eyes pleading with them for absolution.

They shook their heads. The first male lifted his clenched fist. "You have stolen from us."

The other three, in unison, called out, "Thief."

The man nodded in agreement with his companions. "You must be punished."

"Hasn't he suffered enough?" Angela asked softly. "You have not given him a moment of peace since he took it. He tried to have it given back. He has asked for your forgiveness. Where is your sympathy? Where is your heart? Can you not find it within yourselves to forgive a foolish human?"

Her comment caused Byron to look at her, confused. Was she saying she wasn't human, either? Was she also a fairy?

"No. We cannot forgive such impudence against us," one of the women said, the others nodding in agreement.

Byron gasped as his companion sprouted thick,

luxurious golden wings that wrapped around one side of him, pulling him closer to her. They weren't the delicate translucent wings the fairies displayed, but more like a huge bird with solid feathers filling the appendages sprouting from her back.

The four fairies seemed to lunge toward them all at the same time, not at all startled by her transformation.

Using one of her wings, Angela swatted one of the women away from them, causing her to stumble backward and into a tree, where she slumped onto the ground, momentarily dazed.

Byron realized his companion's wings were strong and fierce against the fairies. He wasn't a fighter, but could handle himself in a bar fight. As one of the males approached him, he threw a right hook and caught the man on the chin, but it only forced him to twist his head slightly from the fist's impact.

"Oh shit," he exclaimed. They may be fairies, but they seemed pretty powerful, barely feeling his hardest punch.

Angela shoved Byron behind her, and as he shook his punching hand from the sting he sustained, he let her protect him.

Using her wings and fists, Angela fought off the four fairies that seemed intent on trying to reach Byron, who was backed up against a tree. Her body more than covered him while her wingspan lifted, forcefully swiping at the fairies. She also used her feet to kick in one direction while her fist and wing went in another.

The fairies didn't give up easily as they continued to try to penetrate the protective field Angela established with her very presence.

The previously dazed female silently moved around the backside of the tree line to attack Byron from the rear, pulling him away from the tree while Angela was focused on the other three, who were assaulting her frontal flanks.

When the woman roughly pulled Byron from the safety of Angela and the tree, she cold-cocked him, and Byron fell on his ass. He didn't have a chance to lay on the ground and recover from the attack before the woman fairy picked him up again by the scruff of his collar, sending a punch into his ribcage. She threw a couple more punches to his kidneys before she allowed him to slump to the ground once again, slipping from her grasp as he kicked her to get away. Byron didn't get to go very far before she scooped him up once again. She was ready to throw another punch at his face when she got a face full of vehement feathers, forcing her to fall back herself. Her head hit a tree, and she remained dazed on the ground.

While Angela had dealt with the woman who attacked Byron, another of the male fairies gripped her other wing, yanking on it.

Angela cried out in pain, immediately trying to tuck it into her body, protecting it from further injury.

The final woman rushed to the fallen female's side, helping up the disoriented fairy. The women then disappeared, leaving Angela, Byron, and the two male fairies.

Standing, Byron moved towards Angela's injured wing, trying to ward off the male who was going to use the injury to his advantage in his attack. Byron tackled him around his waist, head butting his gut as his arms wrapped around the male's body. He felt the gossamer wings flutter against his arms but tried to not think about the feeling that he was attacking some giant insect.

Pulling his arms away after they both landed on the ground, Byron used what advantage he had to pummel the man, striking his face and body with as much force as he could muster, oblivious of the pain shooting through his hands from the assault, or his body from the woman's earlier attack.

While Byron was dealing with the one male fairy, Angela focused on the last remaining fairy. He was just as focused on her.

He made a frontal attack, to which she allowed him to get close enough before she sent a powerful punch to his nose, satisfied as she heard the resounding crack as it broke. He yelped in pain and backed away, his hands covering his face.

"Goshin. Let them go. For now."

The fairy with the broken nose disappeared immediately.

Goshin rolled away from under Byron and immediately evaporated, leaving Byron to swat the air where the male fairy had been but moments before.

When Byron realized he and Angela were alone, he scrambled to his feet and turned to her. "I'm sorry about your wing. Is it bad?"

"It's pretty damaged. It has been a long while since I've had to physically fight," she said softly, pulling her wing to her as she checked it out, wincing with her own touch to the injury.

"Come. We need to go. My time grows short. I've only a little time left since daylight is approaching, and I cannot protect you here any further when the sun rises."

Chapter Four

Moving to her uninjured side, he slipped his arm around her waist to help her to walk. She seemed weak as a result of the battle, and he had the feeling there were a lot more punches to her that occurred without his knowledge. He was sure there was some mental combat between the fairies and Angela as well. She looked overly worn and debilitated, more so than just physical exhaustion.

Of all the nightmares he had, this was by far the oddest one.

He helped her away from the area. "I don't know how to thank you. I'm not sure where to go to get out of here. You know, your name is very appropriate. You've been my angel, helping me against god knows what. I'm sorry you got hurt."

"I know. I'll be okay. A good day's rest and I'll be as good as new. I'm not an angel, though. Far from it, actually."

He chuckled. "You've been too kind to be a devil. Wherever did you learn to fight like that?" He helped her sit on a large fallen log nearby. Although it was covered with moss, he took his shirt off to help give her something dry to sit on.

She was grateful for his kindness, sitting and examining her wing to see the full extent of the damage.

Not sure what he was looking at, he tried to peer at her injured wing, as well. "It doesn't look broken, but I'm not a doctor."

"I don't think it is. I can still move it, albeit painfully. Tell me. Why are the fairies so angry with you? What did you take from them?"

He sighed, sitting on the log next to her, not caring that the dampness seeped into his jeans. "I didn't think they were real, so I took a stone from a fairy ring we visited just before I left Ireland."

"We? Are you married?"

"We, as in the group. I was traveling with as part of a guided tour. As for being married, I was. I'm divorced. She found my best friend a better companion than myself. We were high school sweethearts. A couple of years ago, she developed cancer. I stood by her through all of her diagnoses and treatments, only to have her leave me for my best friend, who also was her doctor. After my wife left me, I didn't know who to trust. I departed Minnesota and went to this village just outside of Chicago. Lombard seemed to be the perfect place for a fresh start. A small-town feel yet close to the big city. Before I started my new job, I took my dream trip to Ireland. I decided a trip to Ireland was the respite I needed after such a contentious divorce and the mental anguish that resulted from my best friend and my wife being together without me in their lives, as well as the toll of moving to another state.

As a history buff, I was intrigued with the tales of St. Patrick ridding the island of snakes, the invasion of the Gauls, later called Celts, and of the Vikings, the great famine, and the war between Northern Ireland and Southern Ireland. I found the peat farms intriguing and fell in love with the scent of it burning. I adored the horse-drawn buggies still used around the Ring of Kerry. I thought banshees, fairies, and leprechauns were just myths, balderdash stories to scare children into behaving. I wanted to prove I was right. Instead, I was shown how incredibly wrong I was. It's just not how I saw my life going."

"One never sees the betrayal of another who is

trusted until it is too late."

"You sound as if you speak from experience."

"I do."

"Want to tell me about it."

"No." She gave him a soft smile before turning back to her wing.

"Are you a fairy too?"

She laughed. "Goodness no. Did you see those wings? A strong breeze would rip right through them."

"What are you then?"

She turned to him, sobering up. "Let's just say I'm your good luck charm." Looking up at the sky, then frowned as she turned to Byron. "It's time for me to depart. I cannot stay any longer, but you'll be safe for now." Angela stood and headed deeper into the woods.

He started to follow, but she turned her head back towards him and shook it, telling him not to pursue her. He held back a moment longer, then continued into the forest of trees that surrounded them, after giving her a moment, regardless of her discouragement to follow her.

He couldn't let her go into the woods alone. After so many of his dangerous exploits in that area, he didn't want her to be facing those hazards alone. She had protected him and was injured as a result. Because of him. He couldn't have that on his conscious too.

However, she was gone. There was no sign of her, and he couldn't fathom how she disappeared so quickly, leaving no trace behind. It made him wonder if she was a fairy despite her claiming otherwise.

Chapter Five

Sitting up, Byron gasped as he realized it was all just a dream. He rubbed his face with his hands. It was the first night in a while that he hadn't woken up screaming from the terror evoked by his nightmares, yet it was certainly a strange dream nonetheless. Honestly, he wasn't sure what to make of it. It certainly couldn't be real, but his whole body hurt as if he had truly tackled someone, and his fist was bloodied as if he had actually thrown some punches. He got up from his chair and headed into the bathroom. Peeling his shirt off, which was slightly damp, he saw bruises forming on his torso. He didn't remember running into anything that would cause a bruise, yet they appeared shaped like a fist. He washed his hands and gingerly stepped into the shower, letting the hot water soothe his aching body.

He wondered if the bruises were real, the pain factual, were the fairies true as well? Was Angela? And if they did exist, how was he ever going to redeem himself to them? Would he ever see Angela again? There was something about her that looked familiar.

Was it his subconscious trying to remember someone he'd met, or was it his imagination of what his perfect girl would look like?

"I know I'm lonely, but this is ridiculous," he told his mirrored reflection as he toweled himself off. "Why can't I be lucky enough to meet someone like Angela in real life?" Once dry, he wrapped a couple of bandages around his knuckles, feeling as though he now looked like some prize fighter coming from the ring.

As he headed out, he glanced at his latest addition, thinking that tomorrow, he would put it on the roof. Then, he stopped dead in his tracks. The face of his gargoyle statue looked like Angela, which was why she'd seemed so familiar to him. "Shit. I'm going crazy. I'm enamored with a fucking statue."

Angrily, he grabbed his coat and headed out to work. Although he realized Angela was only a stone figurine, he couldn't help thinking about her and the talk they had after the fight or how she handled herself on the battlefield, doing her best to protect him.

At work, he became pensive as he reflected on Angela the entire day and could not wait to come home and examine the statue once again. She had told him she was his good luck charm, and with the bit of peaceful rest he had, despite the bruises his body sustained, she seemed to be just that. But was she real or only his imagination? Would she come back to him in his dreams? Would that be the only place he could be with her? He was anxious for nightfall, eager to see if she would appear again, and he yearned to be with her, to find out more about her, wondering who she was and if her wing had healed, then criticizing himself over his own imagination.

Once he was at home, he quickly fixed himself a sandwich to eat along with a bag of Oreos, then sat down with the gargoyle statue on his dining room table for companionship. "I don't know if you are real or just a figment of my wishful thinking. I don't know if I will see you again tonight, but I hope so. I hope your wing has healed. I hope we can talk more. I'm anxious to find out more about you. Who made you? How are you able to come to life? I've heard gargoyles are lucky, protecting those who have them on their housetops, yet you seemed to have helped me without being on the roof of my home."

He looked at the mail he had brought into the house with him after work as he finished up his sandwich. "All I get are bills and advertisements. I remember the days when people got letters. Funny how I haven't thought about that for a long while. I guess I'm far lonelier than I originally perceived. Not only am I talking to myself, but I keep thinking about you. I've lost it, I guess." He pulled a larger envelope from his mail and frowned. "Shit." He held the package up and waved it in front of the gargoyle. "This is the fairy ring stone. They returned it to me. It looks like it was opened and resealed. Guess they don't want to touch the stone either. I can't go back to Ireland and return it myself. I don't know what to do." In total despair, he put his head down in folded arms on the table.

He didn't know how long he had remained like that when he felt a soft hand on his shoulder. "We will find a way to return it and garner the forgiveness of the fairy folk."

Slowly, he lifted his head, sighing. "I'm dreaming again, but I'm glad you came back."

"It's not a dream. None of it is."

"Where are your wings? Are you healed? What do

you mean this isn't a dream?"

"Well, for one, you're not asleep. For another, I'm mostly healed. It's still a bit tender, but the wings only appear when I want them to."

Byron looked to the table, but the statue was gone. "You're the gargoyle, aren't you."

"Yes."

"How?"

Angela sighed softly. "May I sit?"

Byron jumped up, offering her his chair. "My apologies. Of course. Can I get you something to eat or drink?" He pointed to the open bag of Oreos. "An Oreo?"

"I'm not sure what an Oreo is." She peered over at the strange, dark, circular object. Was she supposed to eat that? "Water, however, would be most appreciated."

"This is an Oreo. A cookie that I'm addicted to. Try one."

He then bounded off to the kitchen and grabbed a bottle of water from the fridge, loosening up the cap for her before he set it down on the table. It was something he did for his wife, who hadn't the strength to open some of the bottles on her own, especially when she'd been given chemo or radiation for her cancer.

"Thank you." She took a sip of the water before setting it aside. "For now, I'll pass on the cookie. In answer to your question, I was cursed years ago. I used to be human. I was in a small county in Ireland about three hundred years ago. A sickness came through my village. My father died of the illness, and then my mother got sick. As I tended to her, being with her through the last throes of her life, my husband accused me of not being with him and our daughter. I wasn't aware that while my mother was dying, my daughter became ill and passed away before I could get home to her. I often prayed at the fairy tree near my property. I left them offerings to protect my family from the scourge that afflicted many in the area. Yet, still, my parents and my daughter perished. My husband then fell ill. He incriminated me as being the cause of the others getting sick and dying since I showed no indications of becoming infirm with the disease. No matter what I did or how I prayed to the fairy folk to save him, he still passed. I was so angry, furious that the fairies did nothing to help me or my kin, that I kicked their fairy tree and swore at it. I fell asleep that night crying, and when I awoke, I was no longer in the village but perched atop St. Colman's Cathedral in Cobh, County Cork. At first, I didn't understand why I was there or how I even got there. I was looking down on the world, and when I moved, suddenly I had wings. I realized I had been cursed by the fairies in retaliation for my ruining their sacred tree."

"Cursed?"

She nodded. "Yes."

"Three hundred years? You must have seen a lot of changes since then."

"I have. It amazes me the technology that exists in the world today."

Sitting down next to her, he looked at the empty space where the gargoyle had sat before turning back to her. "You're so beautiful," he murmured. "Sorry."

Angela smiled. "It's been a long time since I've heard anyone say that. Thank you." Sobering up, she pulled the package to her. "The thing about fairy rings, like the trees, is they are also sacred spaces. However, I can take us anywhere, even back to Ireland, in order to return the stone. I believe there is a ritual that must be followed when putting the stone back that will incur their forgiveness and release the curse they put on you."

"And your curse? Can you be released from it?"

She looked at him, surprised. "No one has ever offered before. I honestly don't know."

Reaching out, he gently cupped her cheek. "I would like to help you however I can. I owe you that much."

She lowered her head, disappointed he only felt like he owed her something. She didn't know why that bothered her so, but it did. "I don't know, and you owe me nothing. However, I can help you and protect you." She stood. "I need to check on something. Will you be alright while I'm gone? I won't be long."

Byron nodded. "I'll be fine. Just be careful," he added, then watched, stunned, as she disappeared before his very eyes. He shook his head and rubbed his face before looking around, realizing it had all just been a dream. It was better than the nightmares he had been enduring, but none-the-less just a figment of his imagination and maybe a bit of Oreo crumbs stuck in his throat.

"Great. I'm absolutely losing it. I'm caring about a piece of statuary, an inanimate object, and I'm talking to myself. I've finally cracked up, and they can put me in the mental institution in the next couple of days."

Chapter Six

Standing, he picked up the water bottle. It was missing some from when she had taken a few sips. She. Like she was real. Flesh and blood. God, how he wished it were true. He wanted to know her, have her be a part of his life, not this imaginary friend he had just dreamed up, but then that is probably why she seemed so perfect.

Walking back into the kitchen, she reappeared, startling him so much he dropped the water, the cap coming off and spilling everywhere.

"I'm sorry. I didn't mean to alarm you." Angela looked around for something to help dry the water from the floor.

Byron grabbed a few paper towels and threw them over the puddles to sop up the wetness. "It's okay. I'm just not used to my imagination being so active."

She laughed. "You still think I'm a fabrication you've created or even that you're still asleep. Yet, you don't have the statue you bought from the antique store on your table or in the hall. You have the bruises and aches from the fighting we did last night, and yet, you still don't believe it. What more proof do you need?"

He shook his head. "Things like this just don't happen."

"You didn't believe in fairy rings, and yet you've been punished by them since you took the stone. Others won't touch the rock to return it to its rightful place, yet still, you don't trust what you cannot disprove. You believe you spilled water and cleaned it up. You believe you took a trip to Ireland and have yet to fully unpack. Yet, you don't believe in me."

Listening to her, Byron knew she was right, even if he didn't want to admit it to himself. He stepped up to her, gripping her by the upper arms, and kissed her solidly on the lips. Pulling back slightly, he looked a bit surprised. She wasn't the cold stone he'd anticipated kissing. Instead, her lips were soft and supple.

Her hands went up to gently touch his face, and she leaned in this time, placing her mouth softly against his.

He pulled her closer, his arms wrapping around her, his tongue asking for entrance. She obliged him, her mouth opening to tangle her tongue against his. A part of his mind questioned what he was doing, but he couldn't help himself. He had found her beautiful, captivating, enchanting, and he prayed she was real. She seemed real to him. Under his touch, her body pressed against him. If he was going to be admitted to a mental institution, at least he was going to go happily.

Breaking contact, he looked deep into her golden eyes. "You seem real enough. I hope you're real. I hope you can help free me of this curse. Yet, I feel lucky that if not for the curse of the wee people, I might not have met you, and I really want to get to know you better."

She smiled at him with a sadness that seemed to emanate from deep within her soul. "I'm not human, Byron James. I cannot be with you. I, too, am cursed by the fairy people, and I'm not sure I will ever be free."

"Have you tried before?"

"At first. I apologized. I fixed the tree to make sure it didn't die. I gave many offerings that went unheard or unanswered. I even petitioned a woman whom I thought of as a friend when I was alive and who tried to help me break the curse but to no avail. I stopped trying after that and just accepted my fate to guard over those whose buildings I adorned."

"How did you end up in an antique store here in the States?" He led her back into the dining room, where they could sit and talk.

"Church renovations. I was sold to other places, eventually put on a ship, and brought over to the Americas. Gargoyles are considered lucky for those who receive their protection, but as buildings were renovated or demolished, I just got moved around."

"In a way, I'm glad. I've always found gargoyles unusual. I know they were created for churches as a way to facilitate conversion to Christianity from pagan beliefs."

"Yes. They served as a reminder of what could happen if they were associated with the devil and hell. Later, it was so people would no longer be afraid of converting away from paganism."

Byron nodded. "I'd found them interesting. Always have. When I saw you in the store, I just had to have you as part of my home. More so when the nightmares started. Speaking of which, you said you could help me escape from them?"

Angela nodded. "Yes. I will help you return the

stone. Are you ready to go?"

"How?"

"Trust me."

"I do. I don't know why, considering I rarely trust anyone after my best friend and wife cheated on me, yet for some reason, I trust you implicitly."

Holding out her hand, she waited for Byron to take it, using her other hand to grab the package that contained the stone. As they both stood, she produced her wings, wrapping them around him.

He surprised her with a quick kiss, and when she looked at him, he smiled. "For luck."

Chapter Seven

Although he didn't feel the wings unwrap from around his body, Byron heard what sounded like wings flapping in the air. One minute, they were standing in his dining room, and the second, they were outside in the grove where the fairy ring was located.

"Don't do anything yet. I need to gather some oak branches. They were considered the sacred tree of the druids and will be needed in offering to break the curse. I gathered everything else we would need and placed it by the ring. There is an oak tree over there." She pointed and started to walk towards the tree.

Byron stood in a stupor for a moment before he quickly caught up to her. "We are really back in Ireland?" He glanced around nervously.

"Yes."

"Impressive."

She glanced over her shoulder at him and smiled. "I never thought so, but then I'm used to it now. See if you can find some acorns. I'll work on the boughs."

Nodding, Byron started to scour around for the tree's seeds. By the time he found a couple, she was done gathering some of the twigs lying around.

Together, they walked back to the fairy ring. "Now what?" he asked, wanting the whole cursed idea to be over with. Yet he also wondered if, when the threat was gone, Angela would be gone as well. He hoped not. He truly had started caring for her, despite the shortness of their time together.

"Now, we go to their space and talk to them. First, put the stone back on the wall. Then, hold the acorns and twigs in your hand as we travel to their world. You will need to beg for their forgiveness and offer them your gifts. Hopefully, they will accept them and free you from your nightly intrusions."

Setting the twigs down, he took the stone out of the envelope she had carried, before he placed it on the wall. Scooping up the twigs while he still had the acorns in his hand, he turned back to her.

She wrapped her wings around him, but this time, he didn't hear them fluttering. Moments later, she pulled her wings back.

The fairy ring was still there, and at first, Byron didn't think anything had changed, but when he looked around, he realized the ring was surrounded by a heavier, thicker forest that he recognized from his nightmares.

She gave him a gentle push towards the ring.

"Hello?" He took an unsteady step. "Hello?"

He heard the flutter of wings, and soon, there were several beings with gossamer wings encircling Angela and him. They all seemed to be glaring at him, and nervously, Byron held out the acorns and twigs. "I'm so very sorry for not believing in you and stealing from you. I brought the stone back, and I offer these to you. Please accept my apology or tell me what I can do so that you forgive me."

The male who had confronted Byron before, in his dreams, stepped forward. Byron recognized four of the fairies that surrounded him but kept his focus on the man who appeared to be the leader. Somehow, he knew their names. The leader was Ruune. The women were Amber and Gem. The other male who was in the grove fighting was Goshin. As Byron looked around each of the crowd, it was as if they whispered their names in his mind. He recognized Spritz when his eyes settled on him, realizing that Spritz was the one who usually gave him that sense of being chased, causing him to run in most of his dreams. He turned back to Ruune. "Please."

"What makes you think we could ever forgive a thief?" Ruune asked.

"Ruune, at least listen to what he has to say. He did bring us offerings." Amber moved next to the fairy leader.

Ruune crossed his arms and gave Amber a look before turning back to Byron. "Say your piece."

Byron looked over at Angela, who nodded to give her consent. Clearing his throat, Byron set the twigs and acorns down. "I didn't believe it. I thought fairies and magic were myths. I thought gargoyles couldn't come to life, and leprechauns, pots of gold at the ends of rainbows, and banshees were just stories. I assumed that myths were just things exaggerated by people ignorant of things they didn't understand, so they told stories to make them comprehensible. I was the one ignorant of all their beliefs. I was the one who didn't appreciate them as more than just stories passed down through the ages. I may appear as a man, but when it comes to all of this," he waved his arms around him, "I'm but a child learning. Please forgive me. I understand now. I've learned." Hanging his head, he couldn't bear to look at any of them despite their beauty.

Although Gem remained further back, she did speak up. "He looks repentant. His heart is true."

"Not all believe in us. We haven't made our presence known as often as in the past," Spritz added.

Ruune looked over at Amber. He needed her guidance, trusting in her the most.

Amber gave him a small smile and a brief nod. "His heart is true," she reiterated.

Stepping closer to Byron, who lifted his head at the approach, Ruune peered at the humble man.

"Forgiveness is a gift of the gods. You have offended us, blatantly abused our property. We're angry and resentful of the acts you perpetrated against us." His tone scornful, Ruune continued with a slightly softer voice, "Spritz is right. We haven't made our presence known as much in the modern world as in the past. Your era, with the electrical magics, scares us. We prefer the simpler way of life, embracing harmony with the grass and trees, appreciating all they provide for us." Sighing, he gave Amber and the others in the circle another look before he continued, "Prove to us you are worthy of our forgiveness."

"How?"

"We would require of you seventeen acts of atonement."

Byron remembered his tour guide mentioned that the Irish had a couple of numbers they considered sacred. Three since one of the gods had three heads. Five, for the five great roads, the five provinces, and the five paths of law. Seventeen was considered a mystical number, with things taking place after seventeen weeks or seventeen years. 'Seventeen acts' wasn't surprising in and of itself, but he knew there was more to come. "What are these acts that you would like me to do?"

"For the next seventeen days, we want you to do a specific deed." Ruune held out his hand, and Goshin ran up to him, handing him a piece of paper. In turn, Ruune handed it to Byron.

Taking the parchment, he scanned what was required of him.

You need to find three four-leaf clovers and deliver

them to our sacred area.

You need to find three horseshoes, spit on them, and throw them over your head for good luck before you bring them to us.

Pick three shamrock flowers and offer them to us.

Bring us five pints of mead and leave them in the ring.

Do three acts of unselfishness, but call out to the Fairies of the Emerald Isle when you do so that we know you did them on our behalf.

He wasn't sure where he was going to find four-leaf clovers, shamrock flowers, or even horseshoes lying about, but he hoped Angela would be able to help him. As if reading his thoughts, Ruune nodded. "You may employ the aid of your guardian. However, everything must be accomplished by the end of the seventeen days." He stepped back, and all of the fairies shimmered away.

Byron was alone in the grove with Angela.

Moving up to him, she silently asked if he was ready to depart. Once she was given his consent, she wrapped her soft, feathery wings about him only to open them moments later in his dining room back in Lombard.

He was quickly learning to not be surprised at this form of travel. After all, he was dealing with fairies, gargoyles, and who knew what else? Byron waved the sheet of paper around. "I have no clue where to begin to do these things."

"I will help. They said I could assist you."

"Thank goodness for that. I'd be lost without your assistance." Plus, Byron realized he would get to spend more time with her. Although the fairies were beautiful, Angela had a loveliness that belied explanation. She was graceful, elegant, and poised. She had eyes that bewitched him and touched his soul. She gave him a peace and calmness he had never experienced before, and he knew she was the best thing that had happened to him in ages. Maybe insulting the fae and finding the gargoyle statue were meant to occur so he could meet and get to know Angela, who otherwise he might never have encountered. "Where do I begin? What should I do now?"

"Although your seventeen days have begun, you might start with a good night's sleep. Since they have tasked you with several obligations, they will leave you alone until your tasks are complete or you fail to finish your trials. However, I will remain on watch while you rest."

Byron nodded. He knew Angela was right. He hadn't had a decent slumber since before he took the rock from the fairy ring and pissed off the fae. "You're probably correct. We can start first thing in the morning."

"First thing at sunset. I only come out in the darkness of night." Angela hung her head sadly. It had been hard to admit she was limited in this form. Three hundred years since she had been human, but her heart had remained true during that time, and over the years, she had forgiven the fae for changing her to what she was now. Unlike in her life, where she was helpless to assist others, she now understood her ability to affect a difference in others' lives by just doing the little things that mattered. She would be remembered by others for protecting them, even when she couldn't be there for her own family.

Chapter Eight

During work, Byron called around to many gardening stores and florists, trying to find someone who carried shamrock plants. He found two in Chicago. He hated the thought of driving into the city, but he was desperate to get the flowers and four-leaf clovers taken care of as soon as possible so he could focus on the other things he was going to have to do. The acts of kindness should also be fairly simple, as there were so many people who needed help in one way or another.

Addresses in hand, Byron headed into the city after work. The expressways were somewhat clear since most of the traffic was coming out of the city, not going into it. His GPS gave him the directions he needed, and thirty minutes later, he found the first shop. Parking was a bit difficult, but he managed to find a space two blocks away. Feeding the meter for parking, he walked down the street to the store.

"Hi. Welcome," a young female clerk greeted him when he entered.

"Hello. I called earlier today and was told you have

some shamrocks for sale."

"Of course. Follow me." She left the register, after locking it with a code, and led him to the outside area. She walked down a couple of aisles before she stopped. "Here you go, sir. We don't carry a lot of them. We don't get many calls for them outside of St. Patrick's Day, but we do have these couple of plants. Can I help you find anything else?"

"No. Thank you. You've been very helpful."

She smiled and walked back to the front. There were three plants, but only one had a flower on it. The rest didn't. One flower when he needed three. Still. He looked over his shoulder at the other two plants, checking them carefully for any that might have a four-leaf clover. None of them had one. Sighing, he picked up the one with the flower. One flower was better than none, and he hadn't really checked this one out for a four-leaf clover. As he headed back up, something else caught his eye, and he scooped it up as well. Paying for the two plants, he headed back to his car. Once settled, he put the other address in the GPS and started towards the second shop.

Fassi's Garden Center had a parking lot, and

Byron was thankful he had a better location to leave his vehicle. Although the place was bigger than the last, finding someone to help him took a bit more effort.

While he walked around looking for help for the shamrocks, he found a plant with a second name that caught his eye. Foxglove, which was also called Fairy Thimbles. He stared at the plant for a few minutes, then thought it couldn't hurt, so he added it to his cart. Finally, he found a worker down one of the aisles. "Excuse me. I could use some help?"

The man, who was watering some of the plants, looked up, turning off the hose. "What do you need?"

"I'm looking for shamrocks. I was told you had a couple in stock."

"Really? I'm surprised we have some this late in the year. They will be in the perennial section. If we still have some, they would be this way." Setting the hose down, the worker led him to the perennial section, towards the back, where it was shaded more. "They don't do well in direct light, so we keep them back here. Well, whaddya know, we do have a couple left. Here you go, sir." The worker pointed them to Byron and then took off, probably to go back to the hose he'd left behind.

There were five plants here. And two of them had flowers. He put the two in the cart, checked the other three for four-leaf clovers, and found none. Looking around, he was going to pick the flowers from the first two, then decided he didn't want to cause problems of any kind. Being thoughtless is what got him in this situation, to begin with. Better to be safe than sorry.

Walking past the annuals, he saw a plant called Fairy Flax. It wasn't pretty, but he decided to add it to his cart, as well, as an additional offering to the fae. Headed to the cashier, he paid for his purchases and walked back to his car.

As he was ready to pull out of the lot, someone caught his eye. In the past, he knew he wouldn't have given the man a second glance and instead would rush past him as he drove away.

Today was different. Meeting the fairies opened his eyes to the circumstances of others. Where he had been oblivious to the plight of humankind, he was now keenly aware of those who suffered around him.

Tucking the plants safely in his car, he headed towards the disheartened soul. What may have started as one of his atonements has since developed into a desire to help his fellow humans. Determined, he had one more mission to compelete before he returned to his abode.

Once home, he brought all his plants inside. It would be dark in another two hours. Enough time to get prepare something to eat. He fixed his surprise package and set the table, then waited patiently for Angela to once again come to life.

Chapter Nine

The sun dipped beyond the horizon, the colors bursting through the sky in pinks, oranges, and a hint of red. Despite the beauty of the sky, Byron just watched the lowering of the solar disc while keeping his eye on the stone statue. He was getting impatient but didn't move away from the table.

When twilight turned to darkness, the statue quivered as if he were looking at it in a heatwave. The stone masonry melted, replaced with bronze feathers and golden bronze hair. Angela stood, stretching her wings as well as she possibly could without knocking over everything in the house. Turning, she saw Byron with a hanging pot of Fuchsia. Tilting her head, she was a bit bewildered.

"Hello. I got you some Fuchsia. I know they come from the southwest area of Ireland. I thought you might enjoy having something pretty to gaze upon during the day."

Reaching out, she took the plant. "It's beautiful. Thank you." She didn't have the heart to tell him the plant originated in South America and was brought to

Ireland a hundred years after she'd been cursed. It was, however, the thought that counted, and she knew it was a very sweet gesture on her behalf. "They're called the Tears of God. I love the purple and pink flowers. I will enjoy gazing upon them when everything is taken care of and I am on your roof."

"Are you hungry? I've not seen you eat anything, but I made dinner for us." Byron gestured towards the table decorated with place settings and illuminated candlesticks.

Tucking her wings back in, she smiled. "I do eat, but I don't need to do so every day. It's kind of you to do this for me. Unfortunately, I don't think it will count towards your three acts of kindness."

"Oh. I already did a couple of those. There was a homeless person. I got him a hotel room and purchased a few meals to be delivered by DoorDash so he wouldn't go hungry. And I made sure to tell the fairies I was doing it in their honor. I'm not sure what I will do for the rest of my selfless acts. As for this?" He pointed to the table, then held out his hand for hers. "I wanted to do this for you. I wanted to thank you in a special way for all you have done for me. I'd still be having nightmares, unable to apologize to the fairies, attempt to return the stone or learn of my penance." He hesitated a moment, then wiggled his fingers with a smile on his lips. "Please join me. We can work on my penance afterward."

Slipping her hand in his, she let him lead her to the table, allowing him to pull the chair out for her. He was being a gentleman, a notion that she'd rarely seen from her lofty venues in these current times. She found his gestures slightly bewildering, but considered it an expression of his appreciation for her assistance and guidance.

"I have water, but I also have tea and lemonade if you would prefer."

"Tea? I haven't had that in so long. I can't even remember the last time. I would like that, please."

Nodding, he dashed off to the kitchen and put the pot on the stove. He got all the gatherings he would need for the tea of her choice, having both a rich tea he'd brought back from Ireland and some herbal teas in his cabinet. While the water was boiling, he brought out the selection for her to choose from. "Which would you like to have?"

"I never knew there were so many choices." She looked them over, finally settling on the tea from the Emerald Isle.

He came back shortly with the hot water to steep the tea with, then produced a steak dinner with potatoes and vegetables. "I'm not the best cook in the world, but I hope you like it."

"It looks wonderful. I can't believe you went out of your way to make me dinner. I'm honored."

"I'm honored. You have done so much for me."

"I will help you complete your tasks. I think after we eat, I will take you to a clover field so you can find some four-leaf clovers."

"I tried to find some today. I went to two gardening stores after calling around to over a dozen and found a couple of shamrocks with flowers on them, but they all only had three-leaf clovers, not four."

She smiled, holding her fork in the air with a bite of steak on it. "That's because clovers are different from shamrocks. Shamrocks will only have three leaves, whereas clovers will have mostly three leaves, and you're lucky if you find the fourth leaf."

"I never knew that. I always assumed they were

one and the same."

"In a way, they are, but in a way, not so much. Both symbolize good luck to those who have them, but only the four-leaf clover is sacred to the Druids and the Fae people. They are the ones who grant wishes when a four-leaf clover has been found."

"I also found some Foxglove and Fairy Flax. I remember someone telling me the former is also called Fairy Thimbles. I thought they might appreciate having a little something extra."

As they talked, they enjoyed the dinner, and when it was over, he brought out the bag of Oreos.

"Dessert." He took one out, twisted it open, and licked the white cream off before popping both dark halves into his mouth. "Try it." He grinned as he chewed.

She watched him closely, skeptical of what he was doing by separating the black and white disks. Cautiously, as she reached into the bag, Angela copied his movements with the round treats. Her eyes widened in surprise at the deliciousness. She instantly understood why he seemed to favor them for a tasty treat. She'd never had anything like it in Ireland when she had lived.

When dinner was over, Angela offered to help clean up.

"No worries, Angela. I'll just put them in the dishwasher, and we can get going if you would like."

"Dishwasher? Such amazing things in this period. I've never really been inside a building or abode since I'd been altered, so a lot of your things are rather new to me. I hear things from the streets, but a lot of times, they are just words I don't understand."

"Anything you want to know, just ask. I'll help you however I can. Come on. I'll show you a dishwasher, the stoves we use nowadays, as well as a fridge. We also have running water in our houses, so we don't need to go to a creek for fresh water. It's all really convenient." Byron started to get up, then stopped. "Oh wait, you have got to see this. These are phones."

"I've seen people talking with them on my perch."

"But did you know they do more than just have the ability to talk to people? They can take pictures, order food, get a car to drive you around, and look up stuff. Let me show you." Byron whipped out his phone from his back pocket, showed her how to work some of the apps, and showed her some of the pictures he had taken while in Ireland. Byron was excited to show her lots of other things, which included a computer and a television.

Slightly disappointed in not being able to explore the modern world and all of the conveniences of the day, she soon realized it was two in the morning by the time they finished.

"Only a couple of hours left before we reach the time I must go back into my prison of stone. Would you like to try and find a couple of four-leaf clovers, or would you prefer to try and find horseshoes?"

"Horseshoes sound hard as we don't really use horses to get around anymore, and I'm sure those that are used for carriage tours or Police Mounties are thoroughly checked before they leave their stables."

"Then it's the stables where we should go."

"Oh. I thought they had to be found on the road or something."

She chuckled softly. "The fae folk are particular, but they aren't unreasonable. They didn't specify that the horseshoes needed to be found on the road, only that they needed to be found, not bought and not stolen. Surely there were be loose, worn horseshoes that have been discarded around the barns. You will be able to use them."

"I am putty in your hands at this point. You would know better than I, and I will follow your guidance." Byron held out his hand. "I'm ready when you are."

Nodding, she produced her wings and wrapped them around him. Byron heard the sound of flapping wings, even though they never unwrapped around him, keeping him safe and secure. When she opened them again, they were standing in a field of clover.

"I cannot help you look. That you must do on your own."

"It's my punishment. My penance. It's as it should be." He figured they were in Ireland since the sun was coming up, and he knew there was a six-hour time difference.

Sitting amongst the clovers, he began to examine all of them to find one with four leaves. It wasn't an easy task, and he understood why they were considered lucky since they were so rare.

Stretching his back and rubbing his eyes, he

looked over at Angela, who was crouched nearby. She kept gazing around, the feathers on her wings blowing slightly in the breeze. He realized she was on guard, protecting him from any that might come his way. She was so beautiful, he couldn't believe she was a stone gargoyle. Shaking his head, he moved over slightly and returned to his task. Pulling one up, he smiled broadly. "I found one." He held it aloft so she could see.

She came over to him and looked at it, then materialized a small trinket box. "Store it here along with the shamrock flowers you said you obtained. You can give them the whole box once it is full."

Opening the box, he put the lucky leaf inside and handed it back to her. "So it doesn't get lost."

Magically, she made the trinket box disappear. "We've been out here for almost three hours, and the sun is about to rise at home."

"Then we should go." Byron stood and brushed off his pants before stepping into her winged space. He couldn't help kissing her as her wings wrapped around him. "Thank you."

She looked at him in surprise. His kiss had been a quick peck on the lips, yet it produced a fluttering feeling in the depths of her core.

She hadn't thought herself capable of feeling such excitement at being kissed, nor did she understand how it was even possible.

She was cursed, a creature condemned to roam the night. She couldn't offer Byron another more than protection and it saddened her.

He had been so sweet, so caring, making her a meal, giving her beautiful flowers to gaze upon when she first awoke from her stone prison, and took the time to show her so many wondrous inventions, yet what could she give him in return? Soon he'd be free from his curse and she'd once again adorn a rooftop only taking a humanoid form at night should the need arise. She couldn't be with him. He was a human living in a world she'd only gazed upon for centuries. She came to the conclusion Byron was only intrigued by her and the kiss was only a social display of his gratitude.

They got back just in time before she had to revert to stone. By her feet was the small trinket box she'd put the clover in. He picked it up and added the three shamrock flowers from the plants he'd acquired earlier.

Chapter Ten

The day seemed to drag on before Byron headed home from work. He'd had no sleep the night before, and his whole body was wearisome and worn. He realized he had a couple of hours before sunset, so he set his alarm and lay on the couch to get some rest.

Startled awake, he was surprised to see Angela crouched in the corner of the room, watching him. He wondered what she thought about when she was so still. "When you are stone, do you see, think, feel?" Sitting up, he peered over at her and then the clock. The sun must have just gone down.

She didn't move, and he wondered for a moment if she was awake and heard him.

"Not really. I know when things have happened around me while I sleep, but I am not conscious of it. I don't dream like you do. I guess the easiest way to explain it is that I'm aware when there is danger and alerted if I am needed. Since most threats come at night, that is when I am awake to defend those who come under my protection." She stood and moved over to him.

"I'm sorry. You must have been an amazing woman in your time. You're so amazing now. I'm not sure I can ever repay you."

"You don't owe me anything, Byron. You purchased me, and I have a job to protect you when I am with you."

He hated the way she was so matter-of-fact about his purchase. He'd been captivated with her as a stone gargoyle but as a living, breathing creature, he was entranced.

He didn't want to put her on the roof. He wanted to keep her with him, even if it was just her in masonry form. He thought about her every moment of every day. He ached to be with her, to kiss her, but he dared not. A petty human was all he was, and she was magical and powerful. "How about a pizza before we go back to the clover field?"

"Pizza? I know not, other than having heard the word."

"Then you are in for a treat." Whipping out his phone, he placed an order. He'd paid attention to what she ate first yesterday and made sure there was an abundance of meat on the pizza so she'd enjoy it, as well.

"I'm going to take a shower. Help yourself to anything in the kitchen. The pizza should be here shortly."

Unsure what to do, Angela busied herself with his things around the house, exploring and trying the various gadgets out. He'd explained everything yesterday, but she was trying to put the words and actions to the equipment. It wasn't as easy as she had expected it to be.

The doorbell rang, and her wings popped out, ready to attack whoever was on the other side of the door.

Byron came out, rubbing a towel on his head, dressed in a pair of jeans and little else.

He took her breath away.

When he saw her, he shook his head. "It's just the pizza. Hide the wings. It's okay." Pulling his wallet from his back pocket, he opened the door, paid the deliveryman, and closed it, holding a large flat box. "Let's eat."

Setting the box on the table and grabbing some paper plates and napkins, he opened the box. "This you eat with your hands, so no utensils."

"I'm used to eating with my hands," she announced, gingerly taking a piece of pizza and sniffing it slightly before she hesitantly took a bite. Tilting her head slightly as she chewed, she nodded approvingly. "'Tis very enjoyable."

They quickly polished off the meal, talking about what it was like in her village with the burning of peat for fuel, the thatched roof houses, the dirt floors. They salted their meat to preserve it, but most of the time, it was fish that they ate, being that she lived in a coastal town.

When they finished off the majority of the pizza, she turned to him, dabbing at her mouth and wiping her hands on a paper napkin. "May we enjoy some of the cookies again?" she asked sheepishly.

"Of course." Byron laughed as he got up and headed into the kitchen to grab the bag, returning with it. There were only a couple of cookies left, and he made sure she had them, refusing them for himself.

Pleased, she devoured the rest of the container.

"I'll get more tomorrow, and I'll dispose of the garbage after we have returned tonight. We should go so I have more time to find what we need. What I need. I'm surprised they gave me so much time."

"Seventeen is a magical number to the fae. However, you should know that their time doesn't equate to yours."

"What do you mean?"

"I mean, to them, it is seventeen days, but in your world, it is only five."

"Are you kidding me?"

"I wouldn't do that. You have three of your days left, including today."

"Then, we better go so I can complete everything on time."

She wrapped her wings around him, and they were off to the clover field.

Chapter Eleven

Scouring the field, it took him a couple of hours to find the other two clovers that he needed. Adding them to the trinket box, she nodded. "We should leave these in the fairy ring for the fae. Two of your tasks are now complete."

Byron yawned as he stretched out his back. "Sitting on the ground is not as easy as I once remember it being."

"You are still exhausted. Even though you have a reprieve from your nightmares, you are spending your sleeping hours trying to fulfill their requirements. Your body is taking a toll from lack of sleep and sitting in the same position for an extended period of time. When your quest is done, and I am no longer needed, you can put me on the roof and get some appropriate rest."

Moving up to her, he ran his fingers along her hairline and jaw as he looked down at her. "Having a chance to be with you is well worth any lack of sleep I am getting. You're all I think about when I'm awake. I look forward to when the sun goes down so I can be with you again. You're all I desire, Angela. I'm not going to put you on the roof of my house. I'm going to keep you inside so we can be together." He leaned forward to press his lips against hers.

Angela capitulated to him. It had been centuries since she was desired, and she could feel his ardor in his kisses. His hands wrapped around her waist, pressing her close to his body. She wrapped her wings around them both as her arms slipped around his neck. When she opened her wings again, they were beside the fairy ring.

His eyes were heavy, his bulge prominent and tight against his jeans. "I'm going to need a minute." He pulled back, taking the trinket box from her hands.

Once he settled down, he went to the fairy ring. He was not about to enter it without the fairies' permission, so he set the trinket box on the stone wall comprising the ring. "Fairies of the Emerald Isle, I've collected both the shamrocks and the four-leaf clovers. Tomorrow night, I will have the mead for you and hopefully some horseshoes."

The trinket box shimmered out of sight, and after a moment of staring at the empty spot, he turned back to Angela. "Is that it? The box just disappears?"

Angela smiled as she nodded. "What did you expect? A bagpipe parade?"

Byron sighed tossing another backwards glance at the now empty spot where the small box had lain and shook his head. "I guess not. Should we call it a night?"

Nodding, Angela beckoned him to come back into her embrace so she could magically transport them back to his home.

Byron felt her wings unwrap from around his body and he couldn't help but feel the coldness left behind when she stepped back. He'd been married once before but even losing his ex-wife hadn't affected him as deeply as Angela did. She gave him hope and a sense of adventure he'd not experienced in his marriage. He knew it would be a strange life but he would rather be with her despite the hardship of being together than to be without her.

His heart pounded with excitement when he was with her and the feeling of loss and despair that overcame him when they were apart was almost more than he could bare. He didn't want her to leave him. He needed her like he had never desired anyone before. Angela was like a drug for him. She intoxicated his very spirit.

Byron had thought he'd gone insane, falling into a stupor over a statue but when she came to life, when she experienced his world, he was completely and irrevocably lost. She had become the very air to breathe and it was more than just her helping him with the fairies. Angela touched his soul. He couldn't lose her. He wouldn't leave her. Byron desired her too much to ever conceive of doing such a thing especially since knowing of the losses she'd already endured.

Making a decision, Byron gripped her hand.

"Stay with me." He pulled her towards his bedroom.

"I'll be stone soon." She hesitated.

"Until then, you are still flesh and blood, and I want to hold you in my arms when I fall asleep. Please don't leave me until you have to return to your other form."

Frowning, she wasn't sure what to do. "It's highly impractical. And unusual. I'm not sure if it's even allowed."

"Allowed? Who dictates what you are allowed to do and not do?"

Hanging her head, she gave it some serious thought. "I guess the wee folk would have the final say since they are the ones who cursed and transformed me."

"Until they say otherwise, I think, as my guardian, you should stay with me and keep me as safe as possible." He moved to her, nibbling her neck as he whispered the words in her ear. Bending down, he scooped her up bridal style once she had tucked her wings away and carried her into his bedroom.

Laying her gently down on the bed, he continued to kiss her, his hands moving along her slightly cool skin. He wanted her like he had no other woman, not even his ex-wife. He used his knee to push open her legs, unsure of what kind of clothing gargoyles wore underneath their gown. He was surprised to find none. His hand touched her womanhood, finding the inside of her nether lips damp to his touch. He wanted to be with her intimately, in a way he knew she hadn't been in centuries. He couldn't even contemplate how lonely it must have been for her all those years without contact with humans other than perched on their roofs, keeping them safe from harm while they slept.

She didn't deserve such punishment. He thought the fairy folk were harsh and unkind in treating her in such a way, and he wanted to give her some respite from her solitary curse. Why couldn't the fairies realize she had been hurting, her grief paramount after having lost everyone who meant so much to her? They should've been more lenient in their punishment, considering what she had gone through.

Byron wanted to give her pleasure, wanted to let her experience the thrill of being alive, and he wanted to be the one to express it to her. She seemed hungry for his touch, her body lifting towards him with each caress. He wanted to take his time to explore every crevice of her body, explore every curve with both his hands and his tongue.

He started nibbling her neck, working his way down to her shoulder. His hands kneaded her breasts as he dry-humped slowly against her core. His jeans must be a bit rough against her soft skin, so he kissed her lips as he fumbled to take them off. He then pushed her gown up and over her head, breaking contact only long enough for him to slip the material past their heads, quickly capturing her mouth once again.

"You're stunning," he whispered against her skin.

Moaning, Angela arched her body towards his. "It's been so long. I'm a virgin in gargoyle form."

"Then I'm extremely honored to be the first for you since your change."

"You don't find it weird? Disgusting?"

He stopped what he was doing and perched above her, staring deeply into those golden eyes of hers that he'd found so bewitching. "No. I don't find it weird or disgusting. Just the opposite. I find you extremely gorgeous, a sensual, desirable woman. I can't ever remember wanting someone as much as I want you, and I'm not saying that just to get your consent for sex. I'm saying that because I want to express my deep devotion and appreciation of you. I still have a hard time believing this is all real. That you're real. That fairies exist, and gargoyles can come to life. No, my sweet Angela. I don't find you weird or disgusting. I find you to be amazing, and I am lucky to be a part of your spectacular, breathtaking presence."

"I've never met anyone like you, Byron James. No one has gotten this close to me or meant so much. Although, admittedly, I was usually guarding public buildings and not belonging to one person who desperately needed my help."

Byron smiled, lowering himself upon her as he kissed her again. Yet one word she said bothered him. . . belonging. He needed to prove to her that he didn't own her, and this wasn't just part of what he thought was required of her.

He gazed at the clock. Shit. It was almost sunrise, and soon, she would once again be stone. Sighing in exasperation and unrequited passion, he rolled alongside her and pulled her into his arms. "Good night, my good luck angel."

Chapter Twelve

Waking up with a stone statue in his bed, Byron got up, lightly covering it as though it might get cold during the day. He knew it was a stupid gesture, but the sculpture was more than a stone carving. To him, it was Angela, a hot-blooded, beautiful Irish lady. He no longer thought of her as the statue but as the figure containing the heart of his perfect idea of a woman. She was sweet, caring, helpful, sincere. She may have had a job to protect him, but he was sure that having gotten to know each other over the past few days, there was a deep connection between them developing. He hoped he wasn't wrong and that she felt the same way about him. Her reactions to his caresses and kisses seemed to indicate she did and he prayed it was true.

It was then he realized something. He wanted her to be with him for as long as he lived. He would take care of her and treasure her. He'd never put her on his roof to protect him once this was over. He'd want her beside him, even if he only had her at night. A brief thought of moving to Alaska, where it was dark for six months, would be an option to give her more time awake.

Did she even want to be with him when this was over? She seemed to last night, but then maybe she was only living in the moment, and tonight would be a different story. He had a lot to think about as he showered, dressed, and drove to work. He realized he had some other things to accomplish and used the downtime at the business to prepare.

He made several stops on his way home from work, arriving just before the sunset. Entering the house, he set up the couple of things he was going to need for the fairies that he had purchased and made dinner for himself and Angela. He thought she would appreciate some fish since she told him she'd come from a fishing village. Heading into the shower, he dressed in loose-fitting jeans and a t-shirt, pulled the statue from the bed before placing it by the dining room table already set for dinner, and waited, only getting up to check on the meal he was cooking.

Returning from the kitchen, Angela was standing by the table. He grinned. "Good evening. I have dinner for us. Let me get it. Sit and relax. I'll be right back."

"Does it include more Oreos?"

"It can," he chuckled. "I made sure to stop and buy more today." He quickly scurried back into the kitchen, grabbed a couple of plates of food, and returned to the dining room, setting one plate in front of her and the other in front of himself. "Do you actually rest when you're in your other state?"

"Kind of. It's not like sleep, as you know it. I'm aware of what is going on around me. I am still a guardian, even during the day. I just can't transform. Most evil that comes during the day is of a human variety, human actions against another person. We, as in gargoyles, we don't handle human atrocities. We deal with other-worldly issues."

"Like fairies."

"Yes. Like fairies."

"Vampires and werewolves too?"

"More like banshees, poltergeists, demons, evil spirits."

Reaching across the table, he grabbed her hand. "You're amazing. I know I've said it before, but I honestly can't think of another word that describes you so adequately." Squeezing her hand, he let her go. "I hope you like dinner."

"Cod. It reminds me of home. How thoughtful. Thank you." Picking up a fork, she stabbed the fish, having it break away perfectly. Taking a bite, she chewed thoughtfully. "It's delicious. However, we shouldn't waste too much time tonight. We still have the mead and the horseshoes to fulfill. Have you been able to do any more acts of kindness in the name of the fairies?"

"I stopped at a liquor store today. Purchased some mead from Bunratty Castle, which is located, and therefore, made in Ireland. I bought seven bottles just to be on the safe side. I also bought some flowers and delivered them to a rehabilitation center to cheer up those who are ill and visited with a few of the older patients who didn't have family to visit them. That should take care of my service in their names. So I only have the horseshoes left, and of course, to deliver everything to them in hopes that I have completed what they have asked of me."

"You've been busy. I'm glad. Who knew you could get Irish mead in America?"

"Technology and electronic advancements have made anything you could possibly want just a computer click away. I remember going to Bunratty Castle during my visit to Ireland. We had dinner there, and they promoted their mead very proudly. It was delicious. I had to call around a bit, but found a store that sold it, imported from Ireland. I didn't think we would be able to get to a liquor store or the castle in order to buy it, considering the hours that we are there and have available to us."

"Good thinking. We can take the Foxglove and Fairy Flax plants and the mead to them when we finish our meal, then hunt for the horseshoes. Time is running out."

"I remember." He chewed his fish thoughtfully. There was so much he wanted to know about her. "What was your daughter's name?"

"Erin. She was only eight when she. . ." her voice cracked. Even after all these years, it was still hard to talk about.

"I'm sorry." He reached for her hand. "I shouldn't have asked. I didn't know it was still difficult for you to discuss."

She shook her head. "No. It's okay. No one has asked me about her in so long that it's easy to forget sometimes. I put the loss of everything behind me and tried to comprehend my new role in this world. I've not thought about Erin or my husband, Connor, in a very long time. I hadn't realized how much it still hurts. How much I miss them." She cleared her throat, taking a sip of the water he had out for her. "Erin was eight. She loved to fish with Connor, who would take her out on the boat for the morning's catch. We would sell the extra fish for an income and store the rest in our own cupboards. Fresh was always the best. As good as this is."

"This is frozen, but I'm glad you're enjoying it." He swallowed another bite. "What did she look like."

"She looked like me. Well, the me before I was changed. She had auburn hair with red highlights that glistened in the sun and big brown eyes. Her skin was pale, but she had a sprinkle of freckles across her nose. She had Connor's sense of humor and smiling disposition. The two of them would laugh, finding the world around them funny and extraordinary. I found them both to be awe-inspiring and tried to take their examples of sweetness to those I met in my path of life."

Having finished their meal, Byron cleared the plates, put everything in the dishwasher, and turned it on. "Almost set. Let me get the plants and the bottles of mead, and we can head to the fairy ring to drop them off."

Angela's wings immediately materialized. She helped him carry the bottles which had been placed in a divided cloth bag unlike anything she had seen before. It made carrying so many bottles easier than she had expected. Byron carefully carried the plants. Wrapping her wings around him, they soon were at the fairy ring in Ireland.

Byron brought the plants and the bottles of mead to the ring, setting them on the stone wall. "For the Emerald Isle Fairies. Please accept these as part of my punishment with a couple of additional items to express my truest sympathy for having insulted you."

The stillness around him was almost unnerving, and then a slight breeze picked up, and the items he had left behind dematerialized. Nodding, he headed back to Angela. "Where should we go to find horseshoes?"

"I have a couple of ideas." Holding her wings open, they beckoned to him.

Entering the circle of her wings, he wrapped his arms around her waist. "You're hard to resist. Just so you know," he murmured against her neck, licking behind her ear. He felt her quiver under his soft expressions.

"Stop, or you will not finish in time."

Moaning in gentle despair, he let her go, and she opened her wings. They were near a stable.

"I figured a couple of stables should enable us to find what you seek. When you find them, pick them up by the bottom of the 'u' and hold them so the two prongs are upright, then spit on them and throw them over your head."

"Got it." He couldn't help giving her ass a little slap as he stealthily entered the stables.

It took thirteen stables to find the three horseshoes needed. Angela's time was almost up when they returned home with the final items requested by the fairies, unable to deliver them. Tomorrow, they would transport the items when time would once again be on their side.

Chapter Thirteen

As they reappeared at Byron's home, Byron knew they had one day remaining to bring the horseshoes to the fae. He was also aware they had run out of time during his search for the horseshoes amid all the stables he had visited the previous evening. He didn't even have time to cuddle with her before the sun rose and converted her back into her stone prison.

Pulling back her wings, they were once again in his living room. He set the horseshoes down on his coffee table and turned to Angela, but she was already back to the masonry sculpture of a gargoyle.

"I'm sorry. I shouldn't have taken so long to find them. We had no time together, and I so wanted intimate time with you. We will have to make the most of the time we have left when you awaken. Good night, my sweet angel."

He headed to his bedroom to lie down for a little bit before he had to go to work. He was grateful he could kind of set his own hours, allowing himself to come in at ten in the morning and giving himself a chance to get a couple of hours of sleep.

At work, he thought about everything Angela had told him over the last few days. Not even a week since he'd met her, he had fallen for her. There wasn't anything he wouldn't do for her, no matter the cost it might be to him. After some extensive consideration, he began making some phone calls and prepared a few things he knew he not only needed but wanted to do.

Soon, nightfall would be here, the sun creating a light show in the sky with a hue of brilliant colors. Watching the sun get lower into the horizon, he suddenly saw the statue become the beautiful woman he'd grown to care for very much. Turning from the window, he greeted her, "Good evening."

"Good evening. Shall we go and complete your punishment?"

"Not yet. I wonder what will happen to you once I do so. Will I ever see you again?"

Angela thought about it for a moment before her eyes met his. "I don't think so. I assume you will put me on the roof to guard you, but even if you don't, there is no reason for me to show myself to you. This will probably be our last night together."

Byron took four steps and gathered her into his

arms, her feathers tickling him with their softness.

"I don't want to accept that."

"It is the way of the world. You have your curse, and I have mine. I wasn't meant to be a part of this world other than as a protection for those whose buildings I adorn. I was cursed for public structures and never meant for private residences. Yet, stone erections don't always last. Mine didn't, and I've been moved from one place to another. Even in the antique store, I wasn't required and didn't really transform. I assume when you are safe, I will no longer be needed and, therefore, will not return to you as I am now."

"Then stay with me. Forget about the fairies and stay with me. I would rather have my nights with you than to be good with the fae and not have you in my life."

"No. I wouldn't be doing my job if that were the case." Angela tucked her wings into her body. "However. Let us have these last few hours together before I bring you to the fairies in time to meet your deadline."

Staring deep into her eyes, he gave it a moment, thinking about never seeing her again. It tore at his heart, but he wasn't about to let the opportunity slip past him. If they only had this night, he was going to make sure it was one they both would remember.

Capturing her lips, he didn't let go as he scooped her up bridal style and carried her off to his bedroom. There was a little ambient light coming in from the other rooms, yet it was dark enough for intimacy. Carefully, setting her down on the bed, he stood back and peeled off his clothes while he watched her dematerialize her garments.

He pounced on her like a stealthful cat, gripping her arms and holding them over her head, making her breasts jut out towards him. He didn't hesitate as he took one of her nipples into his mouth. His free hand he used to play with her other breast, kneading and pinching her nipple. He could feel the cold hardness pucker under his fingers, and she moaned, arching into his body.

Wiggling her hips against his, his hardness thrummed against her thighs. He didn't want to let her hands go, but he wanted to move down her body. Lifting his head up, he looked around and found one of his ties from work. Grabbing it, he wrapped it around her wrists, tying them to the headboard. Once he was sure she was secure, he slowly made his way down her body, licking and nipping until he reached her apex. He stared at it for a moment, letting his fingers delve between her lips, feeling her wetness. He used his hands to push her legs further apart and dove into the delicacy that was her.

She tasted like nothing he had ever enjoyed before, and he realized he could spend an eternity just eating her out. He had to hold her hips down as she groaned, twisting as his tongue plunged into her womanhood.

Angela's eyes were closed as she enjoyed every moment of him enjoying his feast of her. He didn't tire, nor did he let up his assault on her core. His tongue flicked in and out of her hole, and when he needed a break, he pushed his finger in, finding her g-spot and rubbing it, causing her to stretch her body against him. While his fingers continued to work their magic, he suckled upon her hard nub. Freeing his hand from against her hip, he kneaded her breast, and soon she was calling his name as she came, her juices squirting from her while he lapped up every drop like a man dying of thirst, having found an oasis. She was his haven, his sanctuary. She had become his everything, and he would do anything to prove it.

He rubbed some of her juices on his cock, already dripping on its own, as he looked down at her. Gripping her ankles, he flipped her onto her stomach, pushed her thighs open once again, and lifted her hips into the air so he could plunge into her. He stopped for a moment, letting her adjust to him and him to her. He could feel his balls twitch against her thighs as he was buried deep inside of her. Slowly, he started to move against her, letting his rod almost come out before thrusting back into her, immersing himself within her depths. With each ramming motion, she would moan in pleasure. He was thrilled he could give her something special, and he intended to make this night as magical as he could.

After pushing into her repeatedly, he focused so he wouldn't come too early and yet wanted her to come again. It took everything he had not to let loose his release, and he had to stop for a moment to let the wave of pleasure pass him by before he started up again. While he stopped for that minute, he began to rub his fingers against her nub. He hadn't wanted her to cool down just because he had to.

She was close, and with his continued, relentless thrusts, she soon cried out again, louder as her orgasm seemed to shatter her. He paused, letting the waves of pleasure run through her body, and then slipped out of her with a noticeable pop. Making sure her hips were still up, he slid under her, reaching up to untie her.

Letting the tie dangle from one wrist, she hovered over him. "You haven't come yet. Why?"

"As men, we have learned over the ages that it's important to make sure women were satisfied before we were."

"So different," was all Angela admitted before she impaled herself on his still-erect cock. "It is your turn to be pleasured." Leaning forward, she gripped his hands, using both of her own to hold him still as she rocked over him, slipping all of him wholly into her wet canal, still dripping with her juices.

Unsure how long he was going to last, he let her do to him whatever she wished. He was putty in her now free hands. She slid her hands along his torso, plucking at his nipples as she rubbed the rest of his chest. Hoisting herself on and off his erect shaft, she managed to have her bottom slap his balls with each undulation she gave him. He'd never known anyone who could do that before, and it was an amazing experience.

Then, she did something even more exciting. She let her wings out, and while she moved against him, her feathers flapped softly, sending a wave of chills through his entire body. Somehow, she made him feel like he was floating above and looking down at what they were doing while, at the same time, he was grounded to her every movement, which was enhanced. "You really are an angel," he moaned.

She laughed softly. "No, Byron. I'm more of the devil in disguise." She propelled herself against him faster, her groin tightening around him, gripping him, trying to milk his orgasm.

He gazed up at her, gripping her upper arms tightly as if to anchor himself from the onslaught of visions and feelings he was going through. Sitting up slightly, he buried his face in her neck, her wings wrapping around them both tighter. He could feel the soft feathers against his sweaty skin. He licked the slight glistening dew off her neck and nipped her ear. "Come for me again, my angel."

He helped her rock on him even faster, and if nothing else, his words were the encouragement she needed to come for a third time. Her convulsions and tightening of his shaft caused him to finally release his hot seed into her body while his face was buried into her breasts. He wanted to wrap his arms around her and pull her tight against him, but he didn't want to hurt her, and her wings were not the easiest to maneuver around.

She tucked her wings away. With her still on him, he scooted off the bed and carried her to the shower, her legs wrapped around his waist. For once, he was going to have company under the water and if he could calm down enough, they were going to be at it again. If not, he still had use of his hands and mouth on her to bring her to fruition a couple more times. It would be his best shower ever!

Chapter Fourteen

They stood outside of the fairy ring, horseshoes in hand. Byron was about to lay them on the wall when Angela stopped him. "We need to bring the last of your tribute to them personally. Are you ready?"

"Not really, but with you by my side, I'm ready for everything," Byron lied, knowing soon he would never see her again, once he fulfilled his penance to the fae.

She nodded, taking his free hand opposite the one holding the horseshoes. Wrapping her wings around him, she kissed him softly.

To him, it felt like a goodbye kiss, and he knew that once this was over, she'd have no reason to protect him further. From what she'd told him, she couldn't protect him from the human condition, only the paranormal ones, and most likely, he wouldn't see her in this form again.

Angela opened her wings, and they were inside the fairy ring beside the grove that had haunted Byron through many of his dreams.

Ruune stepped forward, holding his hand out for the horseshoes.

Gem, Amber, and Spritz watched. Ruune then handed the horseshoes to the three of them. The horseshoes dematerialized from their hands as they began to move around the couple, circling them.

Angela, who remained slightly behind Byron in a guardian stance, became more defensive as the others took up their positions, her wings arching slightly, ready to swat away any who came too close.

"He's not done," Spritz commented matter-of-factly.

"He's outta time." Amber's iridescent wings flapped slightly.

Angela peered at Byron quizzically. She was under the impression that all of the tasks had been completed. Was something miscalculated? Did they overlook something in their anxiousness to end the curse? Had they wasted precious time focused on each other and neglected to fulfill all the fae's requirements?

"I know. I know. I have one more act of kindness to perform." Byron stepped away from Angela and closer to Ruune, who seemed to be in charge.

"He has until the sun comes up or goes down or something, doesn't he?" Angela could get him to do something as an act of kindness, surely, in the allotted time left.

"That's only in a few minutes." Gem bounced lightly into the air and hovered.

"Not enough time to go and come back." Amber's wings fluttered faster.

"The curse remains." Ruune nodded decisively.

"Wait." Byron held his hands up in surrender. "I planned on my final act of kindness to be done here."

Ruune tilted his head questioningly as he waited for Byron to explain.

"My kindness is also to ask for a favor." Byron took another step forward as Angela looked confused. Asking for help or favors from the fae usually didn't end well.

"What is the favor?" Spritz folded his muscular arms across his chest.

"I want you to take away Angela's curse. She's been punished for over three hundred years." Byron shook his upheld palms, indicating he was not done when it appeared Amber was about to interject. "I'm willing to take her place. Set her free and curse me instead."

Angela loudly gasped. "No! He doesn't understand what he's saying. He doesn't know."

Only then did Byron turn around to her, gripping her upper arms. "I know. I know you've watched the world go by, that you've lost everyone you loved, but it's time for you to be alive again. To venture off into the world, not hang on some building guarding it from evil spirits. Let me take your burden. Let me help set you free." He looked into her amber eyes, pleading silently with her.

"No," she repeated. "You can't."

"Yes, Angela. It's time you're free from your curse. You did so much for me, saved me from an endless torment of nightmares. I can do this. I want to do this. I've thought about it, and yesterday, I went to the bank and my attorney. The house and my bank account are also in your name. It's yours. All of it. I want you to live in the world. Explore it. Taste the foods we didn't get to try together. Do the things you've seen but could never do. Travel. This world is so easy to get around and explore." Byron squeezed her arms tighter.

"That's very generous." Gem was impressed.

"Very," Amber agreed.

"What about you? Your life? Your work?" Angela breathed shallowly.

"I've no one who will miss me. Work is just a new job. There is nothing for me except you and we can't be together, or so you said. So, I'd rather live with you having your freedom than to stare at you in your stone form, alone." Byron ran his hands up and down her arms.

"I don't think you realize what you are asking," Ruune tried to reason. "Your curse wouldn't end, and you'd be condemned to be a stone statue. If damaged or destroyed while you're stone, that damage or death happens to you. It's not an easy way to become immortal."

"I'm not doing it for immortality. I'm doing it because I want Angela to be free." Byron dropped Angela's arms and turned back to Ruune. "What has Angela done that she's been cursed in such a way? What was so awful that she should be condemned for all eternity? She prayed to you and asked you for help, not for herself but for her family," Byron's voice continued to rise. "I'm not doing this for a chance to live longer than a human or surpass death. I'm doing this for her and only to give her a chance at a full life that had been cut short so long ago." His voice softened, "In these past few days, I've seen her blossom, be excited about seeing and doing and even eating everything this world has to offer. I can't take that away from her now. I've nothing in my life worth as much to me as giving her a chance to be free." Byron sighed, lowering his hands to an open pleading gesture. "Please. Grant me this favor, and let this be my act of kindness."

"No," Angela whimpered. A part of her wanted what he was offering, but she didn't want to take it from him, and she couldn't comprehend why he would do this for her.

Ruune rubbed his chin in contemplation. "Done."

Angela almost crumbled at his feet but remained on her shaky legs. "Why? Why would you do this?"

Her wings evaporated and appeared on Byron, who was taken aback by the weight of the feathers.

"You are released from your curse, Angela Murray, of the sea settlement. Your burden goes to Byron James of the new world."

Angela closed the distance between Byron and herself. "Why? Why would you do this for me?" Tears were beginning to stream down her face.

Byron didn't answer her question. Instead, he turned back to Ruune. "Thank you."

"We have instilled everything you need to do and how to accomplish it in your mind. It will be like second nature to you." Ruune stepped back, and all four fairies were gone.

Byron realized they were back outside the fairy ring in the modern day. He also felt a tingling go through his body. "The sun is about to rise. It is time I took you home."

She was shattered, collapsing against him, crying on his shoulder.

He wrapped his new-found wings around her and whisked her back to his home. Even though they were back at the brick abode, he didn't want to let her go. He held on to her as she cried.

"Why? Why would you do this for me?" she kept repeating over and over in a hushed, broken tone of voice.

Pushing her back, he looked down at her, then

gently kissed her lips. "Because Angela. I want you to be happy."

"Why?"

"Because I want to give you the chance at a life. And maybe a chance to find someone who brings you joy."

"Why?"

"Because."

"Why?" Her voice was now a whisper.

"Because. I love you." She looked up in surprise, only he was no longer there. Instead, he was at her feet, a brown, stone gargoyle.

Chapter Fifteen

Angela wasn't sure what to do. She had learned a lot of things during their time when she was able to visit. She had watched the world go by throughout her punishment, but it was different to observe the changes from afar than it was to be a part of it. Byron made her a part of it. He cooked for her and ordered pizza, allowing her to try a food that was so foreign to her. He showed her innovations that she'd only heard whispered about from her lofty existence.

Now, she was truly in the world and had no guidance, no one to expand upon her limited knowledge. She wanted to be here with him. Instead, she was alive for the first time in centuries, and he was the masonry statue.

Lifting him off the floor, she peered at his features. There were obvious differences, most notably the wings, but his face still had that strong jawline and slightly skewed hair she'd come to recognize as his look. His eyes still held a soft gentleness belied by the strength of will and character he had shown throughout their few experiences together.

She spent the rest of the day watching him, waiting for the sun to go down. She barely ate, barely slept, biding her time until the darkness enveloped the area, and she had to turn on the magical electrical lamps. Still, she waited, hoping he would transform so she could talk to him, tell him to rescind his request, and let her once again become the creature of the night she was so used to being.

Nothing happened. She wasn't threatened by evil spirits or magical demons, and therefore, there was no reason for him to metamorphose into a living being. She was sorely disappointed.

A week had gone by, and every night, she waited and hoped she would see Byron again, but to no avail. Every night, she would talk to him and tell him what her day had been like, the things she did. She thanked him for the money he left for her. She went to the grocery store for the first time and found it a bit overwhelming, but she picked up the Oreo cookies he liked. She signed up for driving lessons so she could get around and used the car service app on his phone that he'd left for her. Still, she missed him, and she missed the days she was guarding the city's buildings.

Finishing a rotisserie chicken she'd bought at the nearby store, she put the leftovers away and took her spot in front of his statue. "I know you won't come to life for me. There is no reason to. I hate that you left me here. Alone. What guidance you gave was not enough, but more than that, I miss you. You didn't give me a chance to respond to your proclamation before you changed. You shouldn't have sacrificed yourself for me, Byron. I love you too. I tried not to admit it, but I do, and what am I supposed to do now that you're not here? It was bad enough that I lost my entire family, but now I had to lose you as well when I wasn't ready or prepared to. I love you, Byron, but I also hate you for leaving me." She buried her face in her hands and wept.

She wasn't sure how long she had remained like that, but it was just before dawn when she stood and stretched. She was slightly cramped. She jumped about two feet off the ground when she saw Ruune and Amber standing quietly behind her.

"What are you two doing here? You startled me."

"Our apologies, Angela. However, you professed your love for Byron. Love is better than luck, for when one is lucky to be in love and to have that love returned, they are the luckiest people in the world." Amber's wings shimmered in the light.

"Love is the strongest magic on earth. Byron gave up everything because he loved you. He didn't want you to suffer your curse any longer and was willing to accept it on your behalf," Ruune stated the obvious. "However, your proclamation has changed the scales of balance. Do you even remember why you were cursed in the first place?"

"Because when you refused to answer my prayers and my husband, parents and child died, I got so angry that I kicked a fairy tree. I disrespected you and your people." Angela glanced between the two of them, totally unsure what was happening.

"You asked us to help your parents and daughter. However, when your husband became afflicted, you only made one pilgrimage." Ruune nodded.

"You didn't save my family. My parents, my beautiful Erin, died because you didn't help. I had gone to the fairy tree almost daily, asking you to spare them. I assumed my time was being wasted on you helping my husband when he became ill."

"You didn't love him though, did you?" Amber fluttered about the room, examining several of the objects strange to her, like the source of light and the radio that was softly playing music.

"Of course I did. He was my husband, the father of my child."

"Not true." Amber came to stand next to Ruune. "It was an arranged marriage."

"True," Angela agreed.

"He raped you on your wedding night." Amber poked the air to punctuate her words.

"It was expected in that era. I should've been more willing."

"You forgave him for that night and every night after, and he gave you a beautiful daughter as a result of your union," Ruune proclaimed softly.

Angela had to think about it, something she hadn't done in eons. "I guess. Maybe."

"There is no maybe about it. You were angry when you lost your parents and child, but you didn't curse us. You kicked the fairy tree, killed several fae in the process, and destroyed their entranceway into this world as well as their home. Do you remember what you said when you kicked it?"

"No. I was mourning the loss of so many. I was out of my mind with grief. I barely remember anything. It was so long ago." Angela frowned.

"Why didn't you take only my husband?" Ruune intoned. "Why didn't you save my parents and my daughter? Why are you no help to those who have prayed and offered tributes to you for weeks? I hope you all get sick and die slowly so that when you lose your loved ones who mean the world to you, you will know how I feel right now."

"You killed my family with your carelessness." Amber wiped a crystalline tear away.

"So for your curse, we granted a curse of our own," Ruune added.

"We knew you didn't truly love your husband, even though you professed to." Amber moved closer to Angela.

"You're wrong. I did love him." Angela shook her head, protesting the allegation to the contrary.

"Did you? Really? You were already grieving for the loss of so many when your husband became ill. You tolerated him as was expected of you and made the best of the situation, but you wouldn't give your life for him. You didn't dream of growing old together or choosing him if you'd had the choice. You liked him well enough. You were lonely, so you remember feeling stronger for him than you actually did.

"We figured you didn't deserve love either and didn't feel the curse would ever be broken." Amber wiped her cheek with the back of her hand.

"And now?" Angela queried.

"Now, it seems I'm back."

Angela gasped and spun to find Byron standing behind her. She flew into his arms and he laughed softly as he picked her up and did a spin with her in his arms before putting her back on her feet.

Byron kept her tucked in his arms, unwilling to let her go. "Is this permanent? Are we forgiven?"

"Forgiven is a strong word." Ruune pulled Amber back. "However, we have removed both of your curses. You may remain together, alive, human, until you both die naturally. I pray that neither of you returns to Ireland with the ignorance you once displayed with our people. Respect us, and we shall do likewise."

"Trust me. I will no longer trash talk or try to prove

the existence of anything mythical again. You all exist as far as I'm concerned."

"And I shall no longer blame others for my misfortunes. I won't let anger get the better of me without thinking things through. I've learned my lesson well. Please forgive my foolish younger self."

Amber nodded and Ruune gathered Amber's hand in his own. "Know it is only your love for each other and willingness to sacrifice for the other that has released you from your curse. Remember your love, for it will be the beacon in the dark days of life."

Amber and Ruune shimmered away, leaving Byron and Angela alone.

She turned to him. "Is this really happening? Are you really here?"

He laughed and pulled her in for a long, deep kiss. "Does this feel like it's a delusion?" he asked, his voice husky.

"No. It feels like the perfect dream."

"Let me show you how real this is." He flung her over his shoulder and walked with her in a fireman's grip down the hall to the bedroom.

ABOUT THE AUTHOR

When Ms. Hawks went back to school for her associate's, bachelor's, and master's degrees, she had already been working for several years in the travel industry. Her original goal was to write history from the perspective of Native Americans, but her first story took a wild curve, and it turned into a paranormal fictional story with the backbones of Native American History and Culture.

She found she loves to write her stories with a bit of truth to them, so one can learn something while delving into a fictional world.

She lives in a suburb of Chicago with her four males. . . her fur-baby cats. She loves to try new foods and considers herself a foodie. She loves to swim and sing. She travels as much as she can to various Author/Reader events and loves to meet new fans and old friends.

Check out her social media sites to follow her.

Website: AuthorLauraHawks.com

X: @AuthorLHawks

FB Author Page: facebook.com/LauraHawks

FB Fan Group; Hawk's Flock

Instagram: @AuthorLauraHawks

TikTok: @LauraHawks87

Made in the USA
Monee, IL
31 May 2025

18321165R00073